PLAYING
the Hand
I WAS DEALT

Pressing Forward

CHANEL BUDD

Dedicated to my family the

Rose
Johnson
&
Budd

In Memory of Edmonia Rose
Grandmother
1938-2002

In Memory of Millie Johnson
Grandmother
1918-1998

Table of Contents

Chapter 1

Childhood Memories

O n a late fall night, living in East Liberty, the Larimer side of town, I was two years old and remember living with my mother, little brother, and grandmother. There was a knock at the door, but no one would answer the door, even when the knocks became louder and louder with a deep voice yelling for my mother to open the door. This voice was a very familiar voice to me although I was very afraid when I heard the voice. I felt the fear that my mother had when his yelling became even worse. My mother never spoke a bad word about this man while I was a toddler because she knew my brother and I loved him due to the innocence we had at the time. This man, my daddy, Everett Johnson is dark brown, about six feet, two inches tall, with bulky broad shoulders. Everett was a very jealous and angry man for a just cause.

No one in our family wanted my mother with him because of the beatings she went through as a young teenage mother. Why did she get beatings just because he was having a bad day or felt less of a man due to his own shortcomings? At this point in my life, I was still too young to understand, so I always wanted to see my daddy or speak with him on the phone just to hear his voice because he made me feel loved. I was told that my mother went out with her sister one day, and when she returned home, all the furniture was sliced up and her clothes were ruined because he had slashed them with a knife. My Aunt Victoria was so happy that she asked my mother to join her that day because, after my mother saw what could have been the end of her life, it was quite the eye opener! Mom retrieved our belongings that had not been damaged and ran out of the house. This had taken us into what would be a whole new life after leaving Everett.

My mother is very pretty with brown skin and huge dimples when she smiles. The third child of five born to Monies Rosie and Bolo Rosie, she was named Marie Rosie after her grandmother on her father's side of the family. My great-great-grandmother, who we called Mother, was an English native who came from a royal family heritage and was Caucasian; her husband was a Black from Virginia. This was a very interesting part of our family; she passed away when I was fourteen. Marie Rosie, my great-grandmother, married an Indian man, Bolo Ho Rosie, and that is who my grandfather was named after. Bolo Ho Rosie Jr. kept my mother and her siblings upset because he was an alcoholic, spending all his time out in bars drinking while also calling himself a player, married to my grandmother and all. This is what drove my grandmother to a nervous breakdown, having five children back to back with no backbone or support from her husband.

My grandmother had it rough from her siblings growing up, being the darkest girl and looking just like my grandfather, her father. Rosa Davis, her mother, and the late Ed Davis, her father, kept the family together

11

no matter what. This side of my family lived to be comfortable in a respectful way. I always loved Marie because I knew she was trying to take care of my brother and me by herself, and since I was a teenager, doing this was a tough job to have. I was named Nellie after my grandmother Nellie whom I love so much. Everett is a junior named after Everett, which I feel bad about because he really is a junior, looking like my dad and mom all in one. We continued to live in the same area because my grandmother's family lived a couple blocks down, so at least if mother needed someone to rescue her from my abusive father, it would not take too long for help to arrive.

A year went passed, and mother introduced Everett and me to her new boyfriend, who at first we didn't want to be around because we had gotten used to having our mother to ourselves with no drama. His name was Tyrone, and he was tall, with brown skin and great with us, always taking my brother and I everywhere like movies, parks, skating, and letting us drive on his lap, which was always fun we actually thought we could drive a car. A few years went by, and we got the news that mother was having another baby. Oh, it took me for a loop because I had to share mother again; my attention was almost gone being the only girl and firstborn was feeling good for the first five years of my life. Then Chameire was born. I had a little brother and sister, which was nice, but I had no attention anymore. Not only was my sister born, but she was born to the man my mother loved dearly. Several years went by, and we moved because the apartment we were living in was too small; being in a two bedroom with five people was uncomfortable for all of us. My mother moved us from neighborhood to neighborhood until we ended up living in Lemington Heights where my childhood began to be bittersweet.

The good thing about living in hood after hood was that I had been meeting all types of children, which paid off for me in my later years. Living up Lemington Heights changed my life because I really didn't have to fight anywhere else we had lived. The Heights was made up of three sections: Schwerner court, Chaney court, and down the back hill was Luzzo court. All three courts were one way in, one way out. Houses connecting with the townhome look a circle in the middle to lead you around and back out. I always managed to have friends who respected me for who I was, but up the Heights it was like you always had to prove yourself. It was the summer of 1986 when we moved onto Schwerner court, and no one was really outside at the time, so I didn't feel out of place at first.

My little sister Chameire was always going outside to see if she could meet some new friends. Chameire was five years old and at the time got what she had set out to do. The only bad thing about it was she would tell these new friends of hers that she was ten years old, which was my age. This one girl came to the door and asked if I was Chameire's sister. I answered her by stating yes, and she then began to introduce herself to me as Chicken. Chicken had light skin with a nice thick body frame and a gap in her teeth. She seemed cool, so I talked to her for a while, and then she became my first friend up the Heights. It is so rare that a five-year-old goes out and brings friends home to her big sister.

I continued to help mother move everything in and get our rooms in order; then I went to Chicken's house to meet her mother and sisters. I started to go outside and over to her house for a while, and Chicken began to tell me who the troublemakers were so that I would not get myself into trouble up there. I was then told that this one family had thirteen family members who liked to fight and would try people all the time. I ended up finding out about that not even a whole month after moving up into the Heights. The Bey family was what everyone knew them by; they were all raised Muslim and were much disciplined in a way I had never seen before. They were the only family at the time I knew of that really followed the principals of the Muslim faith, in which it truly was hard being children. I only really focused on two of the girls from the Bey family, Honesty and her older sister Angel, a major part of my childhood.

Everyone knew each other up the Heights and always managed to get into it with each other and then speak again with in a day or two. I was the oldest of my family, which it was hard for me. I couldn't tell anyone about all the he says–she says stuff that was going on all. I could remember was what Chicken had told me prior to meeting everyone else. The new girl in the court had to get initiated by fighting a random stranger or girl from the group. I was the new girl, so I chose to fight this girl who wanted to hang with us. All the way through the fight I was nervous and praying for strength to beat the crap out of her or anyone else who would try harm to me. The girl I fought was a very nice, pretty girl. After the fight I took her in my house and aided her from the marks I put on her from the fight. I felt bad, but it was part of the initiation.

The prayer worked for me because I was taunted every day, having to fight after school. Everyone would take turns to see if the girls would be able to beat me up or not. Chicken would be upset—she knew it was going to happen, but she didn't say anything because she had been through all this for years before I had moved up there. My neighbor, Total K-Aus, was handsome, and all the girls from Homewood would envy me because he was my next door neighbor. Many would befriend me just to see him when they came over my house. Total K-Aus favored Special Ed, no exaggerating!

These girls named Crazy D and Little K were also in my age group, and we were cool, too. Angel, Fats, Wanda, Lynn, Charmaine, and Pumpkin were all older than the rest of us, so they would stay out of a lot of stuff unless it pertained to someone older or more than one person trying to jump in the fights. There was a gang in the neighborhood at the time called the D-Train posse, and that was more of a worry for the older children because the D-Train posse were all real street fighters and would fight until they thought they beat you completely down. When summer ended I had a whole new outlook on life, and my future being that I was the oldest and had many fights over the summer just from being the new girl living in a new place, had my guard up for anything! My mother knew what was going on, but her focus was on Tyrone and bingo. That was her life at the time.

Years were going by fast, and life surely was getting worse. Tyrone was starting to go out more, and he had been a home guy, always there cleaning and cooking for my mother while she worked. Tyrone had a construction job when my mother first met him, but I

17

can't remember him working much while he was with us. When he started to go out to the streets more, the attitude in him was changing. He became more irritable with my brother and me. He stopped spending time with us like he used to. Chameire was his only child, so he let her get away with everything. Tyrone would have my brother and me at the dining room table, playing chess games, and wouldn't let us go out to play or anything until the chess games were over. He loved chess and wanted us to love the game also. I told my mother his attitude was changing, but she just took it as we didn't want to see her happy. So mother had to learn on her own that something just was not right with him anymore.

It was the first day of school for us, so I got dressed and ready for school, feeling good because one thing for sure my mother always made it a priority for us to have the best of the best as far as clothes and new shoes. My hair smelt fried from the flat irons and spritz we used when the hair stylist gave us a fresh hairdo. When I got to school, I started looking around, noticing I knew other children from my old neighborhoods, so that made me feel comfortable. Then I heard R-Gone's voice, that is, Little K's brother from up the Heights. His mother had brought him there on the first day of school, too, so I was really excited! Indeed he acted like a big brother to me, too. R-Gone was always starting trouble up the Heights just because he had nothing better to do. None of the girls really liked him at the time. He'd throw chicken bones at people and talk about them to their faces and stuff like that, but I liked him for some strange reason.

Anyway, the school we attended together was Schiller Classical Academy on the north side of town. It was about thirty minutes from my home, and people from the Hill, North Side, Lamier and Lincoln went to this school. So I knew a few and began to befriend many. I really liked Schiller; they had a choir and I loved to sing, so I was able to get out my feelings through singing. School was my outlet, and I loved making good grades, doing it to make my mother proud! I was always a smart girl with a lot of ideas to get ahead, but no one could see it, or they did see it and didn't want me to shine through. After school I would get off the bus, and someone would want to fight me, being that I went to a different school.

I couldn't defend myself when the he says–she says stuff would be going on at the school everyone else went to from our neighborhood, so when I got home, I'd fight and then go in the house do my homework then wait on my mother to get home. This routine went on for a while until the girls got tired of me kicking their butts because of someone else instigating fights. Then one day after school, the phone rang. I picked it up, and it was my mother telling me that Tyrone was on drugs, and she would be home after a while. I heard the music playing in the background, so I knew she was in the bar.

My grandmother would stay with us off and on when she was off her medicine or going through mental depression. Grandma was very sweet, though, and loved all her children and grandchildren. Somehow I managed to get through it all until my mother became an alcoholic herself, leaving Tyrone due to drugs was harder than anything I think she had to do in her young adult life besides leaving Everett. Tyrone was there helping her for thirteen years, and within the last one or two, he was gone to the streets, addicted to crack cocaine which ruined the family we had. This took my mother to a whole different level. Bars, bingo, and work became my mother's new way of living, and with all this said, I became the keeper over my family. I was always a happy child no matter what, but going through all these life changing trials were hard for me.

Neighborhood friends were always there, but it was a shady, never-ending battle, as well. Chicken and her sisters were the strongest friends I had because their mother was an addict, too, so being around them gave me some kind of security whether it was positive or negative. I grabbed onto them because they managed to always try to live beyond these circumstances. Other girls from up the Heights had parents who were single, too, but they were taught to only take care of family, and helping others was not in their nature. I truly believe that they were hurting in their own way, too. There were good times up the Heights, such as our community days when Angel and Honesty's mom would conduct talent shows and dance contests. All kinds of food would be sold, and everyone would get together. I liked being a part of that because it made everyone smile.

Crazy D's house was fun; her mother was a big James Brown fan, so we would watch his videos and dance to them and stuff. Crazy D liked to pull out big knives when a fight was going to break out. I liked that, though, because I always pulled out steak knives, so seeing her remind me of myself. Little K's house was cool; her mother always made their house smell good with incense, and they had nice furniture, too. The boys were always getting into something. My brother Everett loved his Nintendo, so he stayed out of the way by doing that. When he wasn't playing Nintendo, he was trying to sell the clothes and toys he had for money or trading them for other stuff with R-Gone. Everett didn't like to fight at first, so he tried to stay around people who were interested in the same things he was interested in. One day, this boy tried to put his name in something, and when they approached him, my sister Chamerie came in the house to tell me. I ran out there so fast to fight those boys; no one was going to fight my brother without going through me.

I knew my brother didn't like getting into stuff, so that really bothered me. I use to call him a punk but didn't realize he was doing the right thing because I was the angry one from going through all this stuff and then seeing my mom fall apart. All I knew was to go for it if someone tries you. My mom took us to church a lot when we were younger, so I knew about the Lord, and I spoke to the Lord through everything. My mom's sister Yvonne was around, but she never let my little cousins come around that much. She had two girls at the time. Dawn and Adel were both born on the same day three years apart from each other. I found out that Yvonne had issues and didn't trust anyone with her girls because of the past life my mom and they went through. They would always pick with her and call her touched. Well, in the long run, that is what ended up happening to my favorite auntie. What's so crazy is as a young child, age ten years old, while sleeping at my aunt's house, I always went through an experience of trying to awake from my sleep and couldn't. I would hear everyone talking or running around while trying to call them, but no one heard my calls. Then I realized that asleep is what I was. I would count to ten, trying to wake up several times, and then I would let myself go back into sleep to try again to awaken.

This would happen to me often as a child, wondering why it only really happened when I went to visit my aunt or over my grandmother's house. Yvonne got pregnant again and had a little boy, Chance, who only lived with her for three years of his little life before being taken into custody by CYS due to my aunt getting sick. I really think someone put something in her drink because she went out one night and came back totally changed. Her diagnosis was schizophrenia, although being an alcoholic didn't help the sickness in her. So my little cousins started to go through rough times, also. I really felt bad for them because they were younger than I was, so fending for their lives was much harder. Dawn and Adel went to the ATL with their father. Chance, on the other hand, never got out of the government system, and then on top of that, they gave him all types of medication, diagnosing him with many different disorders of which I feel the only true disorder he had was post-traumatic stress disorder from being taken away from his mother and sisters.

See this had me wondering what the heck was really going on. All of a sudden everyone in my immediate family's life was falling apart. No matter how I saw it, you couldn't get the adults to get it together for anything in the world. My grandmother was very intelligent, looking at her children in disbelief, causing their children pain and suffering for their own selfish reasons. They were looking for love in all the wrong places instead of facing the issue at hand and moving forward. It seemed they wanted to soak in the past for an excuse to continue to act out in such a harmful manner. The pattern of brokenness was unavoidable in the hood. Back in these days, you had to go to the church; the church wouldn't come to you.

Of course, our parents went every few years or wouldn't go to church at all because changing themselves of bad habits or old habits was too much of a task. Time didn't wait for any of us; it seemed that there was not an end to the madness. Everywhere you turned, all you'd see was unhappiness and pain.

The good thing was being around people just like you going through the same struggles or worse so that they became a true family for all of our youth in the hood.

Chapter 2

Teenage Blues

L ife went on as if it were normal; preparing for school was great. You still had to worry about dealing with all the haters, and of course, the girls were doing the hating. High school was drawing nearer, and I wanted to go to CAPA Performing Arts School because singing was what I thought I'd do as a career. My mother got me signed up, and I had to audition, which I did and made it into the school! The school was nice. All of the core classes were done in the morning, and then your skill classes were done in the afternoon. All the students in the school had talent, and that made me feel like I was going somewhere.

One day I was coming home from school, and my friends asked me why I was going to CAPA and not Westinghouse with all the neighborhood kids. I asked my mother to transfer me with my friends from the neighborhood, so we could all be together. At first she said no. Then I started to beg her daily until she gave in. After being transferred to Westinghouse, my teenage life took a turn for the worse. I traded singing for smoking, good grades to skipping school, and friend's houses to visit, who were skipping, too. I lost my virginity at fifteen to a boy I thought really loved me. He chased me for a whole school year before I gave in. It was not love at all; he just chased me until he got what he wanted, but I really didn't love him anyway.

My boyfriend had a friend that I liked and thought was cute. I started talking to him and went on a date with him, which I shouldn't have done! He told my boyfriend he was sleeping with me, along with my little cousin, which was his cousin, too, from different sides of the family. My cousin, Bria, was also my god sister whom I had lost contact with. Her mom was on drugs really bad, so she ended up living with her grandmother.

How I met up with her again was crazy. I was calling for my boyfriend, and Bria answered the phone asking who I was.

When I told her Nellie, she hung up the phone on me, and then eventually called my house for me, asking how I could mess with her cousin. At first I felt bad, but then I realized that I had no bloodline with him; it was just that both of us were her cousins on different sides of the family. Needless to say, I didn't have a boyfriend long after that, and what do you know, my now ex-boy-friend started making a lot of money and driving to my hood to show me what I was missing! I didn't care because my new boyfriend had the most money in like almost all the neighborhoods at that time. Somehow I managed to have all the balling boyfriends.

My body was nice with the biggest breasts you ever could imagine! I had dark skin and was all of five feet, six inches tall, with dimples and a smile to die for. I really think that is why so many people hated on me. It was not my fault I was well endowed at a very young age. Yes, I made a huge mistake by leaving CAPA to follow after my friend's man; they were into all types of stuff that I was blind to. By no means did I think to follow my own dreams at the time. Westinghouse had a reputation of having the best band in the city, and all the boys were the toughest on that side of town. The other hood that was rough was the Hill. Those boys would always have fights with Homewood at Kenny Wood Park in the summers.

My hood was the best, though. We were a small section close to Homewood and Larimer, and we teamed up with Homewood because we had more friends there, and we all went to the same school. My mother and her sisters went to Westinghouse when they were young and won Miss Black Westinghouse there. I did join choir at Westinghouse, but it was not at all the same to me. My grades were falling, and I was not putting any effort into it at all. Boys were all over me for real, and I didn't really like anybody but started talking with two or three at a time. Please don't judge me. It was better than putting your trust into one that would hurt you anyway. I saw too many women hurting over men who promised to love them only to abandon them for another woman or drugs—whatever the case—and left them lonely with and without children.

My dad was on the Hill, gone off heroin and crack cocaine, standing on the street corner of Centre Avenue looking just like a zombie from *Tales from the Crypt*. I never looked at him for what he was at the time; I was just wanting him to acknowledge me as his only daughter. It was amazing to me, seeing so many lives lost to crack cocaine. Looking at life from a teenage point of view was scary at the time, due to the adults being so lost.

In 1991, gangs started in Pittsburgh, Pennsylvania. This really made my life a living hell. At first it was really fun because our neighborhood got together just to kick it. There was a lot of smoking weed, rapping, and making of gang signs to use against other color gangs. Then it got worse in 1992; other neighborhoods wanted to fight us and then shoot our people, so drivebys started happening on a daily basis. The news would flash this person and that person died by the hands of another by gun violence. From then on, so much blood was shed that no one thought it was a game anymore.

My little cousin Bria was always up under me, not knowing this was not what she should have been around. I was young myself, two years older than Bria. I didn't really think anything of it; all my friends had been older than me, anyway. Bria looked up to me in more ways than one; she even talked to some of the guy's friends that I had been dating. We almost got the beatdown from older women in the hood and everything. Still, it never once stopped us from doing what we wanted to do.

One day in the summer of 1993, we got word that somebody was laying on the street of lower Lincoln from another hood, shot dead. Bria and I went running down there to see who it was, only to find out it was our own cousin lying on the ground with one of his braids down the street from his dead body. This was the first time in our lives to see a real dead body. After that, it was all the time. When I look back to the day it started, I shake my head. Fights were just fights before that, and we would still see each other again. Gun violence took friends away from friends, children away from mothers and fathers, and siblings away from siblings.

Westinghouse could not have a reunion for the classes of 1993–1995 due to the majority of the guys being deceased and several girls deceased as well. This gang crap was really devastating, due to some of my family being from the Hill and also Larimer, which was a rival neighborhood for us. All I could do is pray and let go. It was truly bigger than me by all means. Life continued to move right along. I started thinking of my dad having a new girlfriend who was my age to say the least and was pregnant with his baby even though he was a drug user. I always wondered about the mind frame of his girlfriend having a drug user's baby and all. What could be done? The baby was going to be born regardless, so I didn't say anything; it was not my place.

My father always talked down about my mother to my brother and me, trying to make it sound as if my mother did a bad job of raising us. At the time I couldn't see it. For real, though, he did a horrible job, and she did a darned good one, raising us without a father in the household. I decided to go and see Everett Sr. just so I wouldn't have bad thoughts against him. I called a Jitney to drive me to the hill so that I could visit my dad, Everett Jr. came along, too. As I pulled up to the projects, there had been over twenty people outside, some hustlers and some drug users. This didn't frighten me, not one bit.

My dad came out to greet us, and there was this tall handsome guy who just wouldn't stop looking at me as I walked into my dad's project hallway. He smiled and said, "How you doing?" I smiled back and went into my dad's apartment. My dad's girlfriend was nicknamed White Girl because she looked white. White Girl was cool with us, after visiting and spending time getting to know us. White Girl's first child was a little girl named Haven. My dad loved her, too, like she was his firstborn all over again. I guess he was trying to make up for not being a father to us by trying it again with White Girl.

After the visit with my dad, I felt good just knowing he was trying to become stable again in his life after fifteen years of being on drugs. The Lord does always answer prayers in his own time, no matter the situation. I left my dad's house and got a phone call a few days later from White Girl, asking me if I had remembered the tall guy who asked how I was doing. He wanted my number, and I told White Girl to give it to him. His name is Lee, and he called me to find out more about who I was, being that I was dressed from head to toe, wearing the gold and mirror door knockers and a French roll in my hair. Oh he just had to know me right?

So we started talking, and he came to see me. Of course he was driving a car. I never dated a man who didn't have a car except for elementary school days. Anyway, I discovered he was not a teenager like me; he was already twenty-three years old. Well it didn't matter to me. I felt like I met a man who would take care of me now, so what the heck, my struggles were almost coming to an end. One day he took me to meet his mother.

She was cool and had other children. His one brother was ten months younger than him, and the others were twenty-plus years younger. He was a grown man, so I questioned that. Then I came to realize that she had been having drug problems and that really damaged Lee, but he never showed his emotions to anyone about her, so I left that topic alone quick. Lee met my grandmother and mom, and they really thought he was just so cute, which he was—six feet, four inches tall, with dark skin and a cunning smile. I came to find out that's pretty much all he was—cute with money. Lee started to give me everything; he always made sure my hair was done and cash was in my pocket. Yes, I loved him just because of that alone!

Young and naïve, I did not know that there was more to him than that. Please, Lee had one baby about seven months old at the time and an ex-girlfriend who was pregnant by him before I started talking to him. No, I didn't let him go because I felt good when he was around me, which was always late night after he got done doing his hustle and of course in the morning. I'd wake up to him almost every morning. Lee was a shy crazy kind of guy, always wanting to tell me how to do everything. It was like his way or the high way which really rubbed me the wrong way! This was one thing I never liked at all, to have someone telling me what to do or how to be. I went with the flow, though, liking it a little bit just because it was like he was showing me that he cared in his own way.

Meanwhile back at the house, everyone was tripping out. My brother Everett was starting to go to the streets like I did, although for boys, it is always harder. Everett was not a fighter unless you took him there, and I mean you had to really push his buttons; otherwise, he was always laid back. My brother used to go everywhere all through Pittsburgh and the outskirts with girl after girl, but then he started getting caught up in little cases, having to go to juvenile detention centers. Charmerie was cool, though she just kept getting into things like I did with the neighborhood girls her age, and of course, after watching her brother and sister, she knew what to do.

Lee kept me busy for a few months until he went to jail for a pending case. I was so sad because I felt as if I had a future with him. His mom told me he was getting all this time because he got caught with a gun, and it was not the case. Lee knew he was only getting a year, and that's what he told me, but at the time I had issues trusting him. That was because I had gone to his mom's house one day early in the morning. I saw Lee's car outside, and his mom told me he was not home.

Ms. Queen would not even let me in the house, so I left with my mother to go to bingo but couldn't concentrate, knowing she was lying to me, so I asked my mom to go back over there. Sure enough, Lee was walking to his car with this girl getting in the passenger side. I asked Lee to come here and give me some money, which he did, and I told my mom to drive off.

I had her drive off due to the fact I found out I was two months pregnant and did not want to hurt my baby in the process of beating him or that chick down. My mom said she was so proud of me for doing the right thing. This started the trust issues in our relationship. I decided to go to his mother's house to get some of his clothes to take to the Allegheny County Jail, and when I got there he had on a crispy white tee looking real fresh even though he was locked up. I asked him when he got that, and he said, "Oh yeah, my baby's mother brought it down here when she put some money on my books." This had me heated for real, so I never went back to see him again! Lee and I were supposed to be, but I couldn't see myself waiting on someone who had two children by two different females and one would not let up, which had me feeling some kind of way.

Then she was pregnant with his child like I was, and she was in his life before me, so I started thinking all types of crazy stuff. This girl was way older than me, and I felt defeated in a way, so I continued to prepare for my baby. No one was really there for me during my pregnancy, so I went with the flow of things. My mother Marie was dealing with this man who was an undercover crackhead who tried to proposition my friend one day when I went to my prenatal appointment. When I came home, she started telling me what happened. At this point, I was five months pregnant. This had me heated, so when he came in, I went straight down to him and punched him in the face for making a fool of my mother. He began to try and hold my hands, and that is when my mother and friend jumped in it; we kicked his butt so bad he was crawling to the front door to get out.

My aunt had a town house in Garfield, so I went to stay there while she moved with my grandma due to being paranoid where she was living. She left me all the furniture and everything, which was good for me. It really gave me time to get my stuff somewhat together before my baby came into the world. When I moved in, I invited Chicken and her sister to come live with me, too, so we could get out of the hood and raise our children without being subjected to all the drama around us. That scenario didn't last long because of this young woman named Tika. She was a little sister to Chicken, for Tika had a hard life too. Tika was brown skinned, very pretty, and had no one guiding her the right way as a young teenager, either. Tika, who was pregnant, too, was trying to take over my house, having Larimer dudes coming in and out. She knew darn well none of the dudes we messed with were from that hood. Also, I was getting tired of all the estrogen flowing all through the house with four females, two being pregnant, one being me. That was just not working!

Chapter 3

Hill District Times

This girl named Judy came by to see everybody, and Judy had a newborn baby at the time. Judy was my girl; we had so many years of being close friends, but she proved to be shady, so I stopped hanging with her for a while. Judy was brown skinned, average in height; she wore glasses and quiet but could have sporadic episodes of clowning and acting crazy. I always knew she was very special but had made some bad decisions, although we all did. See, one thing about me is I started not to trust Judy because some of her other friends were not my friends, and my number one rule was don't ever mess with your friend or family's man.

That's exactly what her friends were doing. Judy asked if I could watch her baby while she went to see some dude from the hill. I didn't mind and couldn't do much anyway, so she went, and lo and behold, I didn't hear from her for the whole weekend. Judy called me and I went off on her and asked her for the address of where she was, so I could take her son right over there. When I arrived it was like a big party going on; the project was full of young men smoking all kinds of weed and drinking. Every one wanting to know who I was.

My attitude was real hood but in a sweet way for me. I was nervous because Lee was from over that way, so I didn't know who knew him or what. There was this one dude there. His name was Nitti. He was skinny and brown, but I seemed to like him a little, so I took his number and left. Lee being gone was taking a toll on me, and when you are pregnant, hormones were jumping off like crazy. Nitti called me a lot then, but Lee was on my mind. I was trying not to get caught up with anyone else at the time of being pregnant, which was so hard for me.

My thoughts were up and down thinking why should I wait for a man who already has two babies? Mine will make three, and he won't have time for me because all these other babies' mamas will be in the picture. Just like the one who came to the jail, she was not giving up easy at all. She was pissed that I was young and pregnant, too. So I let my emotions get the best of me and started to go see Nitti at the spot, which was like a party every day. He was staying with his boys because his mother was on drugs and never kept a place to live. My big heart always had me feeling sorry for some dude who had it bad. Nitti's boy was cool, and that is who Judy was seeing, so I was able to just fit in with no problems.

It seemed like everybody was smoking crack in the early '90s for real as far as the adults go. Being a teenager for me was scary. Where was the future for us when all the adults are so screwed up? Was it good that Nitti and I ended up hitting it off? I liked him but couldn't really get into him because, honestly, it was just something to do at first. I was reacting off of hormones and wanting someone to really love me.

Lee was told when he called me one day that there was someone I had been talking to. It was hard for me to say, it but there was no better way of telling him this but by my mouth. People need to realize that he says– she says talk is horrible, and nothing gets accomplished that way. Being real and truthful means everything, no matter how much it hurts at the time. That's the way I would want it in return; you have to respect the truth.

Nitti's mother did not like me at first, but that ended really quickly. I got an apartment on Burrows down the street from my father. Of course, his mother wanted to live with us because she had nowhere to go when she wasn't getting high. I let her, his sister, and her niece live with us for a while. His sister had a two-year-old deaf daughter, and she was only sixteen at the time— younger than I was. It tripped me out that their lives were worse than mine, and I was complaining. Oh no it was ugly on the hill. There was drama in the projects all day and all night; it was like the movies. People had jokes for your butt and would have you laughing until you started to cry all at the same time. I feel that there are way too many talented people lost without hope in

Pittsburgh that really should be millionaires, but no one showed them the way. Even I had all kinds of ideas on how to get rich, and most of them are now someone else's big break, such as mixed chips, clothing ideas, and even rap songs. Dreams are lost in the midst of the hard-knock life!

It was hard to live with another man, knowing he was not my child's father, but I really didn't want to bear a child with no man at my side. I felt I deserved that much. Nitti sure enough was there during the four remaining months of my pregnancy and three years afterward, as well, until he got into some trouble on the hill with some guy and went on the run for a short moment, due to shooting the guy in self-defense. Oh yes it got real crazy. I started to go through the same stuff but worse because now I have a baby and am going through worse things than I went through when Lee left. The girls on the Hill were crazy and real sluts. Everyone was doing every one with no care in the world at all, and the dudes would talk about every last one of them daily.

The Hill boys were dogs to the heart with a whole lot of money. Nitti was about five feet, eight inches, with light brown skin with a nice grade of hair. He had a crooked nose bone that I did not like but was able to get over it. Nitti, who was a thug instead of a moneymaker, didn't have much, and it made me like him more. See before, all the guys I dated were moneymakers to the heart, and I felt that their hearts were on cash flow so much that time to love someone was out of the picture. I did not realize that even the thugs were dogs, just without the money, but Nitti managed to get me some no matter what, even when he didn't have much. I couldn't tell because he gave it me. All his boys would talk crap because they knew I had a man before him that was my daughter's father, so the threat was there which he was so afraid of. I told him, "You take care of me and be sincere, and you don't have anything to worry about.

The damage was already done when I left Lee while pregnant with his child. I knew in my heart I couldn't go back to him because he would dog me so bad, so I just chilled with Nitti. To me it was the right thing to do because there was only one dude in my life after my daughter's father. Lee really despised me for years to come due to my leaving him and especially for someone from the Hill even though he didn't know him at all. It was just the thought that his boys would have something to say about it. Pittsburgh was so small, really almost everybody had a baby by the same man or woman. Seriously it was to the point where everyone had to make sure that there was no kinship before dating. Nitti had an aunt who lived in California who wanted him to come down for a while due to all the trouble he had gotten himself into, so he would not be killed in the city streets.

At first his aunt Katie told him not to let me come down there; she thought I was just another hood rat. Nitti told his aunt if Nellie can't come, then I am leaving so she agreed to have me stay also. I told Nitti to go because this was my outlet for a better future, raising my daughter Morgan, my love. Having her made my world greater. Moving to California, not knowing what to accept was a much better risk than staying in the hood, watching life sucked right out of everybody, due to the poverty, drugs, and gang violence. Nobody wanted me to move away, but it didn't matter to me because I wasn't getting any support living there! This was to be a gain in my life, being eighteen years old with a baby who was eight months. This was my chance to do the right thing, which was a true blessing from the Lord.

Chapter 4

California Days

Nitti went down first, and then two weeks later, I arrived in the beautiful Palm Desert, California, where the skies were real low, and palm trees were everywhere. It was like heaven to me. The malls had celebrities everywhere, and the nightclubs like Zelda's had poles and cages. It was so different, and for once I could rest without the sound of gunshots. My baby was my number one priority, and I looked at Nitti as being a tool the Lord used to start shaping me into the woman I needed to be for his child. I gave Morgan to the Lord when she was first born. This was something my mother told me during my pregnancy by giving her back to the

Creator after he had blessed me to have her was the best thing. I knew Morgan would always be special, so pretty and chocolate with nice hair and a soft voice. Morgan needed to be nourished the right way instead of what I had to go through in my life. Having a child when you are still a child is the hardest task in life, and seeking guidance from the Lord is the key to success in parenthood. Nitti's aunt Katie was the one I needed in my life at the time, and I did not know she would assist in shaping me into a good mother while coaching me to continue my education. Katie took me to the College of the Desert to sign up for my GED, which I passed it on the first try.

I was very smart but just let go of myself because of the stress we were raised up in. Katie is biracial, with very pretty long hair. The mother of four adorable boys, she had moved to California to get away also from bad relationships with the wrong type of men. She also wanted to change her life. Katie was the perfect woman to learn from. I was taught how to cook more meals, decorate, shop better, and dress my daughter like a princess in baby dresses instead of cute pink girl clothes. My life started to become not a dream but a reality for change and growth. All my childhood dreams started to become a picture in my head again, for I had honestly started to forget that little girl in me from all the pain of living in the hood.

Chapter 5

Everett Moved to California

I loved every day I spent in California, but not long after being there, my mother called me to say Everett was getting into trouble with the boys from Lincoln. I told Katie, and she said he could come down there with me. When Everett arrived, he was dressed all in blue and needed a haircut. After being gone for six months and then seeing how everyone still was the same, tripped me out. I immediately took my brother to get a fresh cut and then we went shopping. Katie had sat me down to tell me how much of my welfare check I had to give her; not only that but I had to give her all my stamps. Oh this pissed me off; I never had someone tell me how much to pay them. True enough, this was her house, but I felt her nephew-in-law was supposed to take care of it. Katie said, no; we women have to do business together! In the long run, this was the best thing that could have happened. She was teaching me to be responsible, so I would know how to pay real rent and not housing low-income rent.

Nitti was starting to smell himself after a while, being that he had never lived anywhere but Pittsburgh, and it was taking a toll on him. Then one of Nitti's boys called, telling us his boy got killed, which really took Nitti over the edge because they were really close friends. I told him to count his blessings; this could have been him easily with all the stuff that was going on. It was just insane how no one could put a stop to the killing. Everett started to find friends quickly, so he would not be in the way, which took a lot of pressure off my shoulder, but it didn't keep him from getting into trouble or going to jail for dumb stuff. My mother had to come down and check on Everett. One time he was tripping out in Cali and went to a party. He lost his weed, although you couldn't tell Everett he lost it. He came to the house, got a shotgun, took it to the party, and made everybody empty their pockets. See, it was crazy because I knew he was that way already. It just worried me seeing him be so aggressive out there in a state where we had no family.

Then Nitti started going out and playing games, trying to be like my brother who was single. I guess he missed doing what he wanted to do himself. This was cool with me because, honestly, I really didn't like him. I was just passing time or so I thought. Then feelings started to grow as he was showing me emotions like crying when I packed my boxes or when I told him that I wanted to end our relationship to go home where all my family was. Nitti started being verbally abusive and then tried the physical abuse, which didn't last long. One night he came in after drinking, wanting sex, and I didn't want to have sex with him. My drive was gone, and Nitti was not a turn-on to me anymore.

Nitti ripped my panties off, smacked me in my face, got on top of me, and started having intercourse with me. As the tears ran down my face, my thoughts were racing on what to do next. Suddenly, there was a knock on the door, which made my day. When I opened the door it was my brother's friend, Shadow, asking if Everett was home. Shadow saw the tears on my face and asked me what was wrong. I told Shadow that Nitti ripped my panties off and took the kitty. Shadow told me to chill and went to get Everett. Nitti left after Shadow did. The next thing I knew, Shadow was back at the house with Everett. Everett was so pissed off. I told him exactly what happened.

Then immediately, Nitti walked through the door. Nitti started getting real defensive and jumped on Everett's back, so Everett grabbed him over his back, and Nitti landed on the floor. Everett didn't even do him like he could have, but I smacked Nitti in his eye twice. Nitti got up after tussling with Everett, spitting blood out on both my brother and me. When he walked to the door, the police were out there, telling everyone to get on the ground. Nitti's eye was closed shut from the two open-handed smacks he received from me. I told the police what had happened, and they took Nitti to jail. Now this is when I started to feel bad because jail is not my idea of taking care of business Nellie didn't call the police on anyone, although five nights of jail gave Nitti and Everett time to cool off and I had peace.

The day after Nitti was in jail, I was watching television, and T. D. Jakes was on with two guys I knew from back home on there, doing a mime show while the broadcast was on. It hit me that prayer had to be what was needed in my life right then, so I started to just praise the Lord. Everett was given an apology for being put into my relationship issues, which really, if Nitti wouldn't have just went for Everett, the two of them may not have even fought. Everett told me I didn't need somebody simple like that in my life. Everett was right, just looking at the whole situation. Nitti inviting me down there gave me opportunities to see sights like when his aunt Katie took me to Las Vegas, Mexico, and Los Angeles where Nicole Simpson had been killed.

Never in my life had I seen parts of the world so beautiful. Being in Pittsburgh and then going to Sandcastle was a big treat. Also I really believed deep down that I had to save Nitti because he helped me when I was pregnant. Yeah, right! How can you save someone who doesn't want to be saved? The only thing anyone can do is pray for them all the time without stopping until the prayer has been answered, if it is God's will in their life. Without the Lord, I learned you really have no one. All those you expect to love you for one reason or the other always have some kind of agenda for being around. Also never expect high expectations for no one but yourself. When you depend on someone to do what you think they're capable of, remember they're your expectations, and they just may not be capable of performing them. Many times people wind up doing it for themselves, anyway. The best person that can fulfill your happiness is yourself with the help of the Lord.

Chapter 6

Time to Do Me

N ow all while I had this drama, Katie was going through some rough times herself. This upset me so much because of hearing all the stories about how he beat her. Then she went back to him after moving the boys away from him to start her life all over. The moment he got out, she went right back to him. At first it was him flying to Cali to see her and then flying her to see him. The boys were terrified at all of this; they knew how he was not only to her but them as well.

My mother told me that she spoke to my uncle D. who was living in Atlanta, trying to get his life in order, being a recovering drug addict himself. I felt maybe moving to Atlanta may be better for my daughter than going back to Pittsburgh. I called my uncle D., and he told me to come out there. We talked about how my relationship was going, and he was very angry, knowing some little thug put his hands on his niece. Katie made sure I got a ticket to move because she was leaving to move back to Pittsburgh with her ex. Nitti was not too crazy about this move, but he knew if I left without him, it was going to be the end of us. My brother left a few months before I moved to Atlanta, so that made me feel good about trying another state.

During this process, Lee had been on my mind more and more, so I called his mother to get his number. He answered the phone, so there was no need to try and get his number. We talked for a while. Lee was asking me why I left him while pregnant with his daughter, but I was already so messed up on mixed emotions, the answers were scattered. Lee was supposed to be the man for me during the early '90s. He was in and out of jail for hustling, and women were all over him. This was not what I wanted for my future, so I told Lee that I would be home sooner than he thought, being that I was moving to Atlanta. It seemed I was getting closer to Pittsburgh.

When Morgan, Nitti, and I arrived, it seemed really weird. Toccoa, Georgia, was a really small hick town with one street full of stores; the rest of the town was apartments, homes, and businesses. My uncle D. was very happy to see us, although when he met Nitti, it bugged him. Immediately he told me that this one was not for me. We stayed with my uncle for two months, and then I was told it was time to get my own place. You see, Uncle D's wife did not really want anyone living with them. Honestly speaking, though, I truly believe it was my uncle who did not want anyone living there; he is like that.

I went to look at some apartments while Nitti was at work, filled out an application, and was approved for the two-bedroom apartment with two baths and a washer and dryer connection. Nitti gave me the money to move in, so we got our clothes and rented furniture the same day that we got the key. We told my uncle D we were moving, and the rest was history. We lived in the apartment for four months, and Nitti just got worse.

This man started going out at twelve midnight, saying he wanted to go get weed. He was snapping out on me for any reason he could find, which really there was not one at all. Morgan was two years old by this time, so I really started to think about her life more than mine, Nitti started saying things like, "Let her dad take care of her" and stuff like that. My eyes jumped out of my head, and that is when I started making plans to pack my bags to go back to Pittsburgh.

No man would ever make me feel like I needed them for anything and then say something about my child like she was a burden; oh no. Nitti would call my mother to try and tell on me as if that would change how I was. This would only make me madder at him, as well as my mother, because she was good for trying to get to me or make me feel less of a person. So I called Uncle D and told him I was ready to move back home. Then I thanked him for allowing me that chance to make a life in that small, depressing town. When Nitti went to work, my boxes were packed, and I was on the Greyhound going back to Pittsburgh. These were the cards I had been dealt, so what could I do but try to play them out. Right?

I got to Pittsburgh with my mother, sister, and brother waiting at the bus stop for me. When I got home, there was a man with my mother, different from the nut she was with before I had left, so I said hello then went straight over to see my niece, Nay. She also won my heart from the very beginning with her light-skinned, green-eyed self. I could not believe my brother had a daughter; this made me proud because he was able to love someone sincerely with no boundaries. Everett was a lot like me, but wanting love sincerely was like asking for a million dollars—very hard to get. Once we were settled in, I started having all kinds of thoughts running through my head like: Oh my goodness, Lee is here. Should I call him? What about Nitti? I know he is really mad I left.

What do you know? I called Lee as soon as I settled down for the night, and he told me to pay for a jitney, so that is exactly what I'd do. When we got to his house, Morgan was so nervous with her hands in her mouth, saying hi to a complete stranger who was not a stranger by any means. This was the day when all my past actions were in my face. Regret was one thing that I didn't have, but pain was all in my bones. Lee really did love me—so he says. See, that is what's so hard to determine because when men are out doing women, love seems so far away. It is when you do something wrong to them that the love was there all along. His mother was cooking dinner when I got there, just a smiling at us. This had to be one of the most exciting times to remember.

Lee was acting real cool though keeping his emotions intact as usual, not letting one bit of how he was feeling leak out. We sat around just talking while watching television. Morgan played with her aunt and uncles for a while, which gave us time to get familiar with each other again. Lee took me upstairs to his room to show all the pictures of us that I had sent him while he was locked up. This brought all the boiled-up emotions from Lee as he went through each picture. There was a picture I had sent him that was taken with lingerie on. Of course, Lee told me that it was given to other inmates because he was so angry with me at the time.

After talking for a while, it was bedtime for all of us, so Morgan went to sleep with her little aunt as I slept with her father in his room. Lee at first was so angry that he didn't want to touch me. All I kept hearing was how bad he hated me for sleeping with another man while pregnant with his daughter. I couldn't blame him for that, but at the same time my hormones were stir crazy! I started to rub Lee's back while he lay on my chest. Then one thing led to another, and we were making love like never before. After making love, tears just started to roll down my eyes. I could not control my emotions, thinking about everything from leaving him to leaving Nitti. My mind was just racing back and forth. In the morning, Lee's mother made breakfast. We took showers, got dressed, and then headed back to my mother's house. In a way I was so happy to be back there because of all the pressure I had felt around Lee and his family. It was hard to face him as an adult, but I was glad to get it over with, though.

Chapter 7

Starting Where I Left Off

The phone rang, and my mother answered it. All I heard was her loud voice yelling at someone. What do you know? She called my name and said, "Get this phone, girl; it is Nitti." When I said hello, all I heard was, "Witch, you left me out here by myself. I can't believe you left me." All I could do was hang up the phone with a big smile on my face because when you take me there, it is over no—more of this stuff. I called Lee. Lee answered the phone, and I told him we were home, so we went over his house. The next evening was even more interesting. Morgan looks so much like him, it was amazing to me.

Lee's mom was smiling, saying, "Look how big you got, Nellie" to which I replied, "You got big, too, Queen." That was a good thing, though, for her. My weight came from the Depo shot given to me while in Cali. I gained almost thirty pounds from getting it. Lee looked me in my eyes with this look of happiness, sorrow, and resentment all at the same time. I could not blame him for how he felt because my feelings were mutual toward him, being a young teenage mother. I really blamed him for going to jail. He had told me there was a pending case against him, but by that time I was in love or infatuated at my age.

Lee had a big afro with a big muscular stature from serving time in the pen for a while. We talked almost all night while lying in the bed, then tears started to fall from the both of us, just thinking back on how it used to be before he went to jail and I left him instead of sticking by his side. The next thing you know, we were making passionate love while feeling so much pain at the same time. After we were finished, Nitti ran through my mind just for a second all over again because I had just left him a few days prior, but this was my child's biological father lying next to me. It felt so good because I really did want him all along. The only reason why I left Lee in the first place was because too many women were in my space. This just didn't sit well with me at all.

Morgan was innocent, not knowing what was going on. Her father was a stranger to her, and it was my fault, so I just kept telling her, "This is your father." Morgan would say I have two daddies, which pissed Lee off because he was her only father even though Nitti was in her life due to my loneliness. You see, being so young, never once did I really think of how our future would be affected. The next morning, Lee took us home but started coming around much more often, which really made me feel good because Morgan was getting what she needed—her real father in her life. Nitti called me almost every day, cursing me out for leaving, as I was trying my best to convince him to stay in Georgia since he loved it so much. Meanwhile I was starting to get back into what was going on in the Burg like all my friends, clothes, and what clubs to go to.

The only down fall of being back was almost twice a week someone we grew up with was getting murdered or going to jail for murder; it was insane. Our city is economically deprived with no hope for the children unless you were born with a silver spoon in your mouth. My mother had taken me to the grocery store so that I could cook dinner; all my family loved my cooking skills. Then we invited my friends over for a welcome-home celebration which was the bomb! All my true girls were there with me and kicking it reminiscing: Angel, Chicken, and Honesty. My mother was happy to have me back, too, but it didn't stop her from looking crazy at me for being who I am. See, one thing about us was that I looked just like my mother, so it really made her take a look at herself every time she seen me.

Mr. Damian was taking care of my mom at the time and moved her from the Heights to a house in the same neighborhood where they both could be comfortable. You could not tell my mom anything at all about her man until he started acting super funny when all her children started being around her. Everett told me that they felt bad when I left them and moved out my mom's house the first time. Suddenly, it felt like my blinders were being removed because the thought never came across my mind even once about how they felt. It was all about how I felt at the time, and being made to be responsible for them was wearing really thin. No one could understand how Nellie felt during all this time except for my grandmother, who was like my mother in my heart and in my mind. She was more of a friend to me than I ever had. Knowing my grandmother had been sick was never a problem for me because she always managed to lift me up, so I thought everyone else had the problem. Meek and mild were the words to describe my grandmother who was always there for me with love which was more than anyone could ever want. It was just I didn't want to burden her with all my problems.

So, the next thing you knew, I was living in a neighborhood; seeing my people one day and dead the next was wearing on me, and having no power to change things kept me depressed. Chameire was getting older now, fifteen years old, and growing up too quick. All the females were hating her, as usual. I told her to always be who she wanted to be, never worrying about what the next person thought of her. One day she came in the house, telling me this girl had a fist fight with her at school over some boy. Oh, this had me hot. It just so happened, after telling me this story later that evening, the girl and some of her friends were walking down my mom's street, and my brother called me to come out side to show me who the girl was. I went straight over to her, and choked her for putting her hands on my little sister. A girl that was with her grabbed me to get me off of her friend then I went off on her.

Everett laughed at the fact that nothing had changed as far as me protecting my younger siblings. Everyone in the burgh was real gangster, even my little sister. I grabbed a hold on to her quickly, though she truly didn't like it because my mother spoiled her rotten. Being that we were not close growing up made it harder for me to get through to her then all that changed. I had to school my sister on the guys, so she wouldn't be deceived although learning on her own is what she had to do. She was always choosing the ones with all the money, but they came also with having all the girls—especially the men that were real flashy. Chameire was talking to this boy who reminded me of the first dude I used to talk to. It was crazy; his family was doing really well for themselves, so that really made me proud.

Anyway, needing employment and housing of my own, I started working at Rite Aid and living in Greenfield. My mother didn't really want me living with her, so she kept trying to find reasons for me to leave. She didn't have to tell me twice, so I got out of there in the dead of winter in 1996. The apartment I got was a shack with very thin walls, but I was happy to have my own place but was scared as hell to live in it. My neighbors were weird as I don't know what, and at one point I thought they had been in my apartment shopping in my refrigerator. Moving in was a slow process, being scared of it, and all I wanted to have someone come with me, but that someone ended up being Nitti's little sister with her two daughters. At this point of my life, it was whatever it was for a while until I was able to really get on my feet.

71

This didn't last too long, but we helped each other as much as possible until it got old. Ki Ki was so into getting her groove on, in addition to smoking blunts all day, that nothing else really mattered not even her little girls. She was totally opposite of me; that was the only thing I did do! A few weeks had gone past, and my mother called to tell me that Nitti was back in town, looking for me. The man had left everything to get back to the Burgh and wasn't even home for two full weeks. Nitti went off with his cousin in an abandoned house, doing God knows what, and the police ran in. The police asked for his license and ran it to find out he had an outstanding warrant for shooting a man who had robbed him a few years back.

My mother had told him to chill once he got here and try to stay out the way, so trouble wouldn't be an issue, knowing we were here also. Nitti did exactly what my mom told him not to do. When the police took Nitti, he called right away. All that came to my mind was how stupid he really was and then I thought he wouldn't be bothering me for a while. Of course, I went to get him a lawyer with the money he had made before getting arrested and to grab furniture for the apartment that was rented in Greenfield. The lawyer was a crook, so Nitti ended up getting five to ten. The dude and his cousin snitched on Nitti with no remorse, which was my first and last time witnessing a snitch pointing the finger at someone.

Crazy times were to follow, being that Lee was in the Heights, made me feel like at least Morgan would have her real father raising her. Lee came to the apartment every now and then to see his child and then it started to be for me as well. His ego was too high to feel like a lame, so we kept distance between us unless I pushed up on him when the mood was right. One thing for sure "no" was not an option, which made the night right every time.

Nitti was at the Allegheny County Jail for a year before they transferred him, so visiting had not been a problem. Everybody was in that jail, including a lot of my cousins and home boys who made Nitti feel more comfortable. Yes, Nitti had a very popular lady on his side, and he let it all go being very immature. This always makes me upset to think about the fact of parents not owning up to their responsibilities with the children so that boys were made to be men at the age of like ten and girls at the age of twelve or so. Then I went making stupid decisions, not thinking deep into my daughter's life while living my own.

The most emotional time during all this was that Morgan was confused, due to Nitti being there for the first two years of her life and not knowing he was not her real father. Then Lee came in as her daddy, which made things overwhelming. It took almost two years more for Morgan to know exactly who was who. Even Nitti had to explain to her that Lee was her real father, after I explained to Nitti that Lee was not the one who made bad choices as far as being a parent. Honestly, there was nothing else to be said. I made the choice in having Nitti come into my life while pregnant, so he had to let it go.

Nitti had a chance to be in our life, and if we would have never left the burgh in the first place, Lee would have been in the picture regardless. Lee had to tell Morgan over and over who he was, which made him hate me more and more each time. All I could do is apologize for what I had done to bring so much pain in his life, thinking of the present with not one thought of the future. Strictly living in the moment that was the mindset for almost everyone in the burgh until this happened to me; it really made thinking a priority. Lee was really being a man, taking care of Morgan and trying to make up for the lost time

Then, all of a sudden, Le was out of the picture. A few weeks went by, so I called his mother only to find out he was back in jail again, too! Violation of parole gave him a whole year to do, which pissed me off and not only me but his mother, too. I found out he had a girlfriend, which kind of rubbed me the wrong way, although couldn't be upset about it. I was upset, though when she called to see if it were at all possible to take Morgan with her on the trip to see Lee. It was a big test, of course; I passed it by saying it was okay to take Morgan.

When Lisa came over to meet Morgan, it was obvious that she liked her for being a very nice person. Lisa stayed for a few minutes and then took my child with her to the jail. It was so strange for me to let

Morgan go only because I would have never done that before, since Lee had been through so much with me. Letting Morgan go made me feel grown up. Never did I visit Lee while he was locked up this time, due to Lisa being in the picture. Seeing Nitti was enough. The idea crossed my mind a few times but no action came from it. Lee called to tell me thank you for letting his girlfriend bring our daughter to see him. Visiting Nitti went on for like two years, but then I started to back off because supporting him was getting old.

My life stayed complicated all the time. Some things I think were done impulsively and some were simply the cards dealt. In 1998 Nitti was transferred to a state penitentiary to serve the five-to-ten-year sentence. This time Nitti had a choice to live right or not, and he chose to risk it all. Thus, it came time to live my life. Employment was easy to get but hard to keep, being that the pay was so little for a lot of hard work. There had been an employment agency someone told me about downtown, so that is how I obtained a position with the Allegheny County Property Assessment Office. The position meant a lot in many ways, such as meeting responsible, well-educated individuals like I grew to become. Childcare was very costly at the time, being a single mother, so moving became the best thing to do.

There were low-income apartments on the hill that were not in the projects. Of course, that became my choice. The apartments happened to be around ten minutes away from work. Angel moved into the building along with my niece's mother, so having childcare was not a problem. Angel, as well as me, didn't play the girls not having proper care, so we looked out for each other no matter what. Playing the cards dealt had to get a full flesh someday; this seemed to be going in that direction. The hangout for us was up Elmore over my cousin Renee's house. It was so interesting up there for real like a comedy show live in the hood. One thing for sure is talent is everywhere. People are given gifts of all sorts, but if you don't get out the hood, it goes to waste; that is what I witnessed daily. The guys were all over the place. Nitti was raised up there, so I didn't really focus on getting to know any of them.

Renee always kept some form of entertainment like parties, girl's night out, and talks about who to talk to and who not to. I love her so much for being real, no matter how her life was going. Out of my father's whole family, she was the only one like me in a few good ways. Renee has four boys, two of them very well-mannered although brought up in the hood; the other two were just as crazy as they wanted to be. The boys played too much with no fear of adults whatsoever, but they loved their mother. In the summer of 1998, Chameire, who was sixteen at the time, came to live with me. The first thing I made sure to do was transfer her to the school district we lived in. I explained to her again how the boys were around the neighborhood, so no one would be able to run game on her. Of course they tried really hard, but only one of them became successful. He was a big-headed, skinny dude, and he took care of her for a long time. Although he was a street dude, the respect level was all right; he knew that she was my little sister.

Chameire is a very pretty girl with a nice build, so I knew all the guys would try to put her on their list. This was not an issue for us because when it came to my people, no one was going to just do anything. The girls would do your man, brother, and father; so would the boys your mother, sister, and auntie; keeping your guard up on the Hill was a must. Charmerie fit right in because until she met other girls from school in stuff, she stayed around my friends with me. One day I went over Renee's to pick her up. This guy was out there looking really good, talking with Renee; we spoke to each other and then went down to the bar. After a few drinks, I asked Renee who the guy was she was speaking with. Renee told me he was cool, but he also was her friend's daughter's father. To my surprise, speaking of Christian, he walked in the bar smiling real sexy with his caramel complexion with a six feet, four inch stature. Christian sat down beside me, asking for my number, buying all my drinks, and the game was on.

Chapter 8

Got My Groove Back

C hristian became my new fling, buying anything I wanted. I didn't even have to ask; he made sure that my apartment had everything it lacked. I thought finally the man has come who is perfect for me, but then Christian started telling all his life stories about how he went to college and then got around to the big information. Christian told me that he used to do drugs of all sorts and was dealing, too, at the time. All of a sudden, my guard went straight up, thinking of all the things I had already been through. I began to observe Christian every chance I got. Renee told me that Christian really liked to be around me, and he would take care of me.

With school time right around the corner, Christian asked if Morgan had all her school stuff. I told him yes, and he still gave me two hundred fifty dollars more to spend on her. I went back to the store to rack up on more shoes, supplies, and clothes for her. Angel told me to take it slow with him because he was too nice, and I took her advice seriously. For some strange reason, tall, charming, sexy, and handsome men were always attracted to Nellie.

These men were very manipulative all the time, and it drove me crazy because it became a pattern in my life to like them knowing it wasn't good for me. One night Angel, Chicken, Renee, Chameire, Lynn, and I went out, and this guy approached me, up in my face, saying, "Yeah, I'm not afraid to talk to you." I couldn't do anything but laugh at him. That pissed him off, but I didn't care what he thought about it. My night went well, to say the least, and then Christian came over when I got home. We talked for a while, and then he told me to take off everything and lay on the chaise. Needless to say, I loved that chaise; it made my love life more romantic than ever before. This went on for a few months, but then Christian started to become a little distant.

My intuition started kicking in, to say the least. I knew a female was somewhere in the mix. Christian knew a little bit about my life except for the fact that Lee was Morgan's father, and Nitti, my ex-boyfriend, serving time in the penitentiary. There was not much he could say to me about anything on a man note. Christian had this girl who my father told me to look out for because she liked to carry knives around her necklace in between her chest. For Christian being in the streets, I guess it turned him on good, but I let it be known that there was not going to be any of that if he was going to continue to be in my life. Eventually, I gave Christian the boot. It was very hard for me, and he always came to visit, but there could not have been any other way for me to go about this situation without getting hurt or someone else getting hurt. Months went on with no man all over again, except for when I needed some loving, Lee came home. That is who I'd always give it up to with no regrets. However, when he got real serious with his girlfriend, I backed off for a long while.

When Lee told me she was having a baby by him, my feelings were so hurt but not as hurt as they became when she had a girl — and then to top it off — he proposed to her. Oh my heart was broken as if he cheated on me or something. Lisa had seen me on my lunch break, walking downtown, and made sure to show me the baby as well as her ring. My eyes were so big because when I laid them on the baby, she looked as if she were my daughter all over again. Lisa made sure to keep Morgan around, which made me feel so much better. After talking to her a few times it came out that Lee told her everything about our relationship and for her not to do the same. I felt she had a lot over me because of this, but it didn't stop me from trying to make a better relationship as a baby's mother to Lee.

Since Lee was now in a committed relationship, I decided to just continue to do me with no if, ands, or buts about it. Not knowing he was still observing my every move, I kept on living my life in a discreet manner, always carrying myself like a lady at all times but not taking any crap from anyone in the burgh. My girl Angel kept me in line when I got carried away. She is quite disciplined, which I admired a lot. Anything she wanted to stop doing, she would stop doing with no second thought. I began to learn more about her when we lived in the apartment building, even though we knew most things about each other from living up the Heights. Angel's daughter was so cute, and the bond they shared was impressive. My niece was a lot like Everett: very aggressive but sweet at the same time. Well, come to think about it, some of that is her auntie.

Morgan, on the other hand, is so not like me in a sense she reminds me of my sister. Morgan doesn't like drama and is laid back and stubborn. This is funny because I believe that is her father to the fullest. The best thing was right in the same building as my child and niece. Then to top it off, my best friend moved into the building with her daughter. Then my father decided to move in the building with his girl, and they're like two children; it went well for a while. My brother Mar had issues stemming from my father's addiction. It drives me insane to know he was using when Mar was conceived, and then both parents act like they don't know why he is so out of control.

Anyway, getting back to my life, I started trying to figure out that my credit was important. I already had bad credit at the age of twenty-two. How was I going to get it back together when all I really had was enough to pay current bills along with rent? Not planning for the future is damaging to a degree, but when you are not raised to value saving, it is difficult to grasp onto after the fact. I was raised struggling and thought this was right because my mom used to say, "I struggled to make it, so you can, too!" This didn't sound right, so I became really defensive when hearing phrases used in such a manner.

Chapter 9

The Struggle Was On

S truggle — now who tells their children to struggle because they had to? Well my mother did, and it stuck to me like glue; I wondered if what was said was truth. I came to realize that life was a struggle all on its own, and surviving the struggle is all that mattered. As long as I had enough or so I thought, living wasn't so bad. There were times in my teen life when I contemplated not being alive. On one attempt, I tried to take a hanger and put it around my neck, thinking if it hangs on the pole of the closet, it could hold me. The hanger didn't budge, and neither did I. Talking to someone would have been much better for that situation, so I went to my mother who took me to a counselor who spoke more than I did. Never again did the counselor see Nellie! Needless to say my thought process was damaged from a child to an adult. I knew what I needed in my life but did not know how to obtain it at all. Moving back to Pittsburgh brought the hardcore life right back into my spirit.

The Hill had every woman losing their religion, fooling with the wrong brothers time after time. All the women knew the brothers were taken, but it stopped no one from giving it up. Even I got a little carried away, dating guys I didn't even really like just to have something to do, classy as can be and gaining respect by the hour just for not giving these brothers any kitty. Brothers were gaining points for being the man, only to have sisters looked at and treated like a piece of meat.

I truly think the role changed with that entire independent woman thing coming to be. In a way it benefits us women, due to having to take care of our children on our own, but degrading our bodies has to stop. Women need to start having much more respect, not only for themselves, but please include other women. The need to stop plucking the other people's eye out without plucking your own is a must. Men became weaker and a lot more dependent upon women. One hundred percent of relationships don't last, due to women playing two roles now more than ever before.

Women, what is really going on with us? The respect we have for ourselves has really come down to none! Why does our own gender downgrade, hate, screw each other's men, accept being called hoes, take being abused, and sell each other short? Start looking at yourself first, and then the need to find probable clause in someone else won't happen as much. This world would be a better place for our children if we women could try to gain respect for ourselves and start encouraging one another. Everyone learns from a woman; there is not one man able to cheat on his spouse without a woman taking part in it. Another issue is that there are so many gay women searching for love through another woman. Come on now; what's up with that?

Honestly I see two women being dogged out going through the same feelings as a man-woman relationship, so why another woman? Nothing changes except for the same old line of "my woman cheated on me." Now how embarrassing, why this can be said because that is exactly what it took for me to find Nellie? No I didn't mess with another girl knew a few of my home girls that did calling me telling me what went wrong in their crazy relationship along with a cousin or two.

After Lee started hanging out again, not being the man at home anymore, I seemed to be paying him more attention. I was thinking if he is not at home with her, things must not be going good for her anymore. An idea came right across my mind to see what Lee really was doing away from home. I was starting to find out Lee had flings that didn't mean anything, but if this was true I could slide in there (that dang devil in my head). So that is what I did; I talked to him for a while just to see where he was, shaking my head because it was so wrong of him to do this to Lisa. And, I wanted him at the same time, rationalizing everything and managing to do wrong anyway! Lee, weak as can be, did what any man would do in the streets; he went straight for it with no remorse. He would tell me how it was nothing and that he loved Lisa, although he was flinging it around at the same time needing a little every now. Again, the satisfaction was all I acquired.

Christian took it upon himself to start seeing this girl with a knife more. I guess it was the thrill of being crazy that got him with her. This was cool with Nellie because she got Christian into some trouble, and then they moved out of town. Knife girl got pregnant soon after the move. I got a call from a lawyer approximately a year after his big move, and the lawyer told me Christian needed ten thousand dollars and was told to call me! Now what would make him give my number like the money was as though I had money. Only an insane person could do such a thing. I told that lawyer there was no one here to give him anything but prayer; his woman is the only one to be contacted.

The reason for the arrest was murder. Christian received twenty-five years in prison—now that broke my heart. Christian chose a crazy street chick, and then his whole life ended that fast because he went from one choice to go another way. He called me a few times and wrote a few letters. The end result though really touched my heart. A twenty-five-year sentence—what the heck is really going on? Then I got the news right after that.

A phone call came in about my cousin who also resided on the Hill. She was very young—eighteen as a matter of fact—stating she just committed suicide due to dealing with an older guy who supposedly had given her AIDS and was cheating on her at the same time. I was so shocked from this. It broke my heart just to see her every now and then, knowing the chance would come for me to speak with her, but then it never did. Seeing her in that casket did something to my spirit. The messed-up part was all the guys looked at that as that was on her, the women started rumors, and the family looked at it as though we should have or could have done something.

Satan is on a prowl for all souls. We really need to pray more and act more as children of the Lord if we don't want to burn forever in hell. It takes one person to make a stand. I'm that person. Let's get busy with trying at least to make the ghetto a better place. As I live each day, trying to make ends meet and working forty hours a week only to have my income swallowed up by waiting bills, I wonder if a man would help make things better. How do you really not struggle anymore when the government keeps your pocket tight? Unless you were born with a talent, it seems you're just out of luck.

Getting back to my home life, I began watching children for my friends and family a lot to make sure they were well kept. Everyone knew that when it came to the children, I didn't play any games whatsoever. My niece's mom said, "Nellie, you fed the children too much," but I answered her by stating three meals a day now are not too much! The proper feeding should include breakfast, lunch, and dinner no later than 6:00p.m. Mothers who don't worry about eating a proper diet to accommodate their lifestyles do indeed have to make sure the children get nourishment regardless. My mom may not have been home a lot, but one thing for sure, she made sure we had a nice house with food in it.

The Hill in my opinion was one of the most active places and more ghetto than any of other places in the burgh. The projects were like mini-jails to me. Everyone who lived there made the best of each day no matter what the day held; laughing was a way to soothe the pain. Laughing at other people's pain made the days go past much faster. Over ten thousand people housed in the projects where there was high crime, drugs, and babies. My thing was how to accept living as if this was normal. Almost no one who lived there really looked very comfortable with living around killings, drugs, abuse, and misery.

Chapter 10

Time to Make a Difference

S ociety is really messed up for African Americans living in the hoods. The only activities being held were in the school, but there was nothing for the children to do when school was out! This bothered me so much that I would sacrifice my own living to make sure the children were safe. Continuing to work full time then after work watching the children for whatever reasons the parents came up with became a routine. Morgan didn't have to worry about Mommy, though, because I was right there for her. I obtained my first car—a Ford Taurus. It was a nice baby-blue color, and I always drove with a licensed driver until I passed the driver's exam. I was so proud of myself, being able to take Morgan were ever she needed to go. Giving Morgan all the attention she deserved was my goal, and it put a smile on her face knowing I was being the best mom I knew how to be. As time went on, I would tell myself that staying focused would give me the drive needed to accomplish all my goals. I wanted to move. Four years on the Hill was just too long for my daughter to be in an uneducated, high crime environment.

The education system was very low for my child compared to when I moved to a suburb. My daughter was now in the third grade, attending a school with the majority being Caucasian children. Morgan's grades dropped so fast I was feeling as if she wasn't getting the assistance at home properly, only to find out the curriculum was much more advanced in the suburbs. I went to her school to speak with the teachers and was told it was the school system's approach that was why my child was not making good grades. Lee started coming over to our new home, which became a great benefit for Morgan. He always drove her to do her best as well as myself. It is something about fathers with children; they listen much better.

Penn Hills was the new neighborhood for determined African Americans. If you moved there, it was because you wanted more in life. Lee really liked the fact that I was driven to do better, and helping me make that move was right up his alley. Leaving my job with the county after my move and starting a new career working at Job Corps, which was closer to my new home, enlightened me on the youth. All these teenagers were troubled teens in search of life, just like I had been. I loved just talking with them and giving each one motivation in their own individual way, which was a blessing. The pay was a decrease from what I was making at the county, but the price of touching the lives of the future made it as if I was getting double the pay.

My girl Chicken lived right next door, so my chilling time was over there with her, drinking on my Budweiser after a long day's work. Chicken would always encourage me as well as Angel; that is why neither one of them left my side since I was ten years old. Having true friends always helps, even when they are doing things you would never do yourself. Being a true friend gives you true friends.

The jobs in Pittsburgh were not paying too much, and time was flying past me. Lee was back and forth. He asked for a key, and of course, he received it and came over almost every night. We didn't call ourselves anything but baby's mother and father. Lisa was also still in the picture, having his little girl and all, which didn't bother me too much after she was born. Lee would talk to me about relocating every now and then, which was right up my alley, being that I had already made that move. No one had ever really left the hood, except for only a handful, so I started doing research to see what the job market was like in other states.

Meanwhile my grandmother's health was not doing so good; she started to use oxygen and then would have to go in and out of the hospital a lot. My sister started going over my grandmother's house often and then eventually moved in with her. My grandmother loved Morgan and Nay so much; she always stated Morgan was her favorite. Something about Morgan's eyes, she said they were dancing eyes. Occasionally we would let the girls stay overnight with her, and they gave her hope, strength, and love, so having them around her was joy for all of us.

My brother Everett started hanging around old friends who were not real gangster. To tell you the truth, he was the gangster out of all of them. Everett always had a good heart, so he would go see these boys just to chill and talk crap with them. One day Everett went over there to visit his friend, and the friend asked if he could run him by the store, so Everett did, leaving his daughter over there while he ran his boy to the store. When Everett returned, he found out the friend's house had just been robbed of legal guns. My niece was told to get in a closet with another little boy who was there while they robbed the place. The fact they had done this while his daughter was there had Everett hot, taking him to a whole different level. A few weeks had gone past, and then one day Everett came over to see if I would keep Nay. For some reason, I didn't feel right about keeping her that day. Everett told me he would pay me and everything, which he doesn't do often, but I couldn't say no.

Later that night, while I was sleeping, my stomach started turning really bad. I started to question whether I was hungry or not, knowing I had eaten already. Then the phone rang. As soon as I said hello, all I heard was someone telling me to watch the news—something just happened. I knew something was wrong with my brother, so I called my mother to see if it was a delusion. As soon as I called, my mom she said get to the hospital; it was your brother. Then the thought my goodness he is the one that got shot in the face I just knew!

When we arrived at the hospital, the nurse told me that he gave my information, not my mother or no one else, but his big sister to contact for emergency, and all I could do is cry. This touched my heart more than ever before. My praying began then anger set in on how the heck someone could try some grimy stuff like this. The boys who robbed his friend's house came back to rob them again when Everett was there. When the boys answered the door, Everett was standing beside his friend when the gunfire started. That is when my brother got shot in the face with a .38. This is what these

99

weird looking boys said at the hospital. They were in the apartment at the time of the shooting.

Meanwhile I went up to the floor my brother was on, and they were rushing him into surgery. I called his name while seeing him in that hallway with blood everywhere and a neck brace on him. He was moving around to let me know he heard me. That day changed my life for good; no one can ever tell me that the Lord is not good all the time. The doctors came in to tell my family he had a 10 percent chance of living or having a stroke, which we claimed to be all in the Lords hands. My father was there, repenting for being a horrible father, but no one could say anything but just stare at him in disgust. Everyone started to come in to the hospital; the thought of this being real made me sicker by the moment. My mother just sitting there a nervous wreck; her having anxiety attacks one after the other just made me more upset. Then my niece's mother came in and brought holy oil in to heal my brother through prayer, anointing his head, with my mother praying as well.

I went in the room one time, scared to approach his room. My little brother—just the thought made me want to go and take revenge. All I could think about was the dude who did this to him for no real reason at all. A little punk did this, and while my brother lay in the hospital, the same boy went out doing more dirt. He got caught with the guns he stole and went to jail where he would meet up with all our family. My brother was released in four days after the shooting and stayed at my house while I tried to take care of him. It was the scariest time of my life, hearing him screaming out for pain medicine in the middle of the night. Then he would get dressed as if he were going somewhere. Now try telling a 265-pound, twenty-two-year-old man to go back to bed. I called my mother, so she could come over to get him. My mother took him to the place where he got shot to help him get over what had just happened and to get his belongings.

To make matters worse, my grandmother was back in the hospital, so then I ended up going to see her. No one told her what was going, but somehow she just knew something wasn't right. All that was said was

Everett got shot, and the first thing my grandma asked was, "Did he make it?" We answered her by stating yes, and then back to how she was doing became our next concern. After everything died down, the dude who shot my brother started telling everybody he snitched, which was not the case. No one ever snitches in our family. The dude was smart, though, because it kind of kept him safe in prison. This really had my pressure boiling, and as soon as anyone asked, I told them the truth.

The dummy kept on doing dirt after the robbery and shooting. He crashed into some other car that severed a man's leg. In the process, the police got the weapons that were stolen from the robbery, so my brother never got to testify. The dude took a plea; my brother wasn't going to testify although he did have to show. One thing for sure is I know the system; every one we knew has been locked up at least one time or another. My brother is a soldier for taking that bullet in the face. One thing for certain, though, is my brother loves the Lord. Grandma instilled that in us when we were young— always trust in the Lord then your days will be long. It is truth that in so many ways, the church will always be our place of comfort and security, not these streets. A few months went past. My grandmother went through many complications from medications to help her fight against diabetes that left her so tired.

Chapter 11

My Pain

My grandmother had to take insulin shots daily to maintain a balance with the diabetes. I did not think much about it because she always had taken the medication, and I did not realize it was coming to an end. My Bible started to become the only comfort I had, so that is where I stayed. For some reason I could not put the Bible down; it was like a few days of this pattern before a call came in, stating my grandmother went back to the hospital again. This time the doctors were saying the other hospital never checked to see exactly what other medications had been prescribed on the last admission. When this was said, I then started to wonder if they were doubling up her medications. As she was only sixty-four years old at the time, death was not an option for my grandmother.

I spoke with my grandmother who told me that the doctors stated when she is discharged she must go to a nursing facility for a few days to check on the lesion the doctors had drained. Being that my grandmother was a diabetic, the lesion had to be cleaned and observed thoroughly. My grandmother told my mother if she went to a nursing home for any reason, she didn't think she would ever make it out alive. My family knew she didn't want to go to a nursing home, but since it was to be a temporary stay, no one thought anything else about it. The day my grandma was being transferred to the nursing home, which was June 28, 2002, we spoke on the phone. Grandma asked questions pertaining to the color of my furniture to the way my home was arranged. These questions startled me although I answered her very calmly with no frustration in my voice at all. It was more of worry due to the fact she never asked questions like this ever before.

After speaking with grandma briefly, the phone rang again. When I said hello, it was Grandma asking more question as well as telling me she was dressed and ready to go to the nursing home. "Nellie," she stated, "I really am afraid to go, but I know I have to."

I then replied, "Grandma, we will be there to visit, and you will be okay. Please call me when you get to the nursing home."

We then hung up the phone, and the day went on. My mother was supposed to go check on her that night. Before my mother could even get to the nursing home, we receive a call just several hours after her arrival to the nursing home that my grandma fell and lacked oxygen to the brain for several minutes, so she had to be rushed to the hospital where she was pronounced to be brain dead. Oh, this really brought all kinds of pain out of me—my brother being shot now my grandma is brain dead and I just spoke with her not even four hours before. Something had to be done; the nursing home needed to be investigated. All kinds of questions were racing through my mind. Did she have oxygen on when she was transported from the hospital to the nursing home? Did the nursing home make sure she had oxygen on her? I truly believe that she had no oxygen on during transfer or after arriving to the nursing home.

My heart was pounding while the tears continued to flow. Chameire screamed and cried, as well, being that she was staying with my grandma during this period of our lives. Chameire just so happened to get smart that same day, so she felt so bad this had happened, never knowing this would be the last time we'd have the chance to speak with our grandmother again. Everett was so selfish when it came to taking care of anyone but himself or his own child, so he just was glad Grandma didn't have to suffer no more. My heart broke into four pieces after the death of my grandma.

Everyone met at the hospital to have a meeting with the physicians about what to do next with Grandma. The hospital kept her on a ventilator until the family could decide on the next move. I believed, because she had movement when I saw her in the hospital, that she could not be dead. I mean, she was moving like someone having a seizure, but it was movement to me. There was no brain activity, so the family decided to take my grandma off life support, but she didn't even pass away until around midnight. From this moment on, my emotions were full of anger, pain, and grief. My outlook on life was very dark. Having Morgan, though, kept me strong enough to start evaluating my life in that present moment.

The first thought was to get out of Pittsburgh again without looking back. Brainstorming became a priority, trying to figure out how I was going to get out of this messed up city! If anyone only knew how bad it was for people who really want more in life than partying, drinking, drugs, and sex. I wanted a real life working hard while earning enough not only for your bills to be paid but to actually have enough to live. Knowing that my grandmother was now gone to heaven made me look at my life to do better to make her proud. I started to use the bad feelings to make good out of it, somehow. Some way, I was going to make a difference in a positive way for my family. Lee would talk to me a lot about wanting to move out of town, but he had never been away from Pittsburgh to live ever before.

Almost all the people in Pittsburgh knew nothing about another state because it seemed everyone was afraid of change. I told Lee to move away before jail or death became his fate. He wrestled with this idea until December of 2002 when Lee finally decided to buy a plane ticket out of Pittsburgh to relocate with his cousin in Florida. This made me so proud of him that I then decided to call my aunt to relocate as well. Chameire decided to go to Atlanta with my cousin Adel to start a new life also.

Chapter 12

Texas: The Lone Star State

L ow and behold, my aunt lived in Texas, so this is where I decided to relocate, not knowing anyone there but her and my cousin Cotton who just so happened to be six days older than me. At first I prayed about the move, and then called my aunt Victoria to get a newspaper so that I could see if there were any Section 8 houses available. When I start calling landlords, at first things didn't go well, so I kept trying until finally a lady answered the phone, stating she had a town home available. After explaining my situation to her about relocating with a voucher, she told me that she is Christian and understands how frustrating it is for a single woman trying to restart her life over and for me to send her the money order for the security deposit. The home would be waiting for me when I arrived in Texas. I then asked my aunt Victoria to please go past it and take a look for me before mailing the deposit. Victoria looked at the town home and stated that it was okay, so I then prepared my move and mailed the security deposit to the landlord.

I spoke with all my family and friends to tell them I was moving again, but this time I was not coming back except to visit. I even offered my home to anyone who felt they needed to get away for a while or what have you. Lee called me every day and night when he finally left the first of January, 2003. He couldn't believe that I was really leaving the burgh myself, but I couldn't take it no more. When Lee left, it felt good because he was able to start getting himself in order finally. Lisa was happy he left, too. She worried just as much as I did about his safety.

Lisa and I got together to get the girls' pictures taken together before we left. Her eyes looked at me as if she already knew somehow Lee and I would join

111

together once we moved from Pittsburgh. The girls' being together was a must, and we put our differences aside for them no matter what. My girl Angel really didn't want me to go, but she knew deep down inside that I would not survive much longer in Pittsburgh. Some can stay headstrong through the storms of the burgh, and some can't I was one with too much of a sensitive and good heart to be able to see everyone losing their souls in that place. People I went to school with were walking the streets, talking to themselves, after losing their homeboys, who were my homeboys, too! Then I couldn't bear seeing dudes strung out on heroin and crack that were my age and girls tricking in the alleys at the age of sixteen years old.

It was time to go for me; that was the only way out. After I spoke with everyone, I planned my move for February 12, 2003, which went very well. I traveled by train while all my boxes were shipped through the post office; I even had the car shipped by dependable auto shippers for a great price. I did everything by having faith in the Lord to direct my path. Prayer became very important to me, but please don't get me wrong; there was still a part of me that drank beer a lot to suppress my pain. Depression was my best friend for several years to come. It was like no one really knew how tired and hurt Nellie became through all these different cycles of tribulation I was enduring.

My aunt Victoria along with her husband are very strict people, not wanting anyone calling after ten o'clock in the evening. This made Lee very upset, being he was the only one who would call after ten. I would laugh all the time when he would finally speak with me because the first thing he would do is go off as if he were talking to my uncle. March 1, 2003, was when my apartment became ready for move-in. Morgan and I could have privacy for the first time in two weeks. We slept on the floor, using comforters and pillows, which was fine by me. She seemed very comfortable lying right beside me. I got a mattress a few days later, but when you are starting a whole new life, sometimes you do what you have to do.

Morgan got enrolled into the third grade and struggled for a while. The teachers had a meeting with me to discuss the possibility to repeat the third grade not because she didn't pass the task test but because they wanted her to learn the curriculum in Texas. The teaching methods were ten times more extensive than in other states, and Texas was known as number one for education. So this then had been brought to Lee's attention in which we both, after long hard thinking, decided that if she would struggle in the fourth grade. So we decided to go ahead and let her repeat the third to get a better understanding on the way the educational system had been here in Texas.

Lee went through some hard times in Florida, which he didn't take to very well. I tried to explain to him that when you leave the fast life to endure a more settled one and do the right thing in life, it seems like everything comes smashing down on you. Every day I would have to give him positive encouragement because he would go off all the time. Lee stated to me before that struggle was a fear for him because of the way his childhood had been, so struggling was not an option. Things became way worse, so I told him to try Texas, which he had been planning to visit any way. At first Lee was hesitant asking for me to relocate to be with him. I told him no due to Morgan already being enrolled in school, not to mention all the time I put in to this major move. The landlord was a blessing; somehow I just knew at this point in my life the Lord made it all possible, so Lee would have to come down here to give it a try. All along, I knew in my heart Lee would try and make it work again.

When Lee arrived, Morgan smiled with the brightest smile a child could have. Lee made up for the time we were apart from each other in more ways than one. After the reunion, months had passed Lee obtained employment. His ex-girlfriend, who was also his daughter's mother, could not believe he moved with me. The phone didn't stop ringing day after day until I told her not to call unless it was about his child. Lisa would call to tell Lee about past relationships, old guys he used to hang with, and anything else she could think of to keep the lines of communication available. Lee got upset with me when I told her that he had moved to be with me.

See, what Lee didn't know was that I saw the old cards, letters, and photos he kept in a box. One day I just had to approach him with it only with the idea to get all of that stuff thrown away—the rest of it anyway. I had already thrown away some of it, especially the ones from other girls in his past. Oh, Lee was hot; he stormed out the house, walking as fast as he could to get away from me for a while. When Lee calmed down, he came in the house and told me that it was wrong to have brought that stuff in here to begin with.

Lisa wrote a letter with no return address, stating if she was the one who would have moved, that is where Lee would have been. That had me so hot that I tried to call her, but of course, she didn't answer the phone. I told myself cowards do stuff like writing a letter with no return address then not answering like a real woman would. In my opinion, Lee was where he wanted to be because if that were the case, she would have been in Florida with him, not him in Texas with me.

Time surely went past, and then his children came to visit us, along with my family. One after the other, my family came to visit year after year. Lee started to get very upset, flipping out due to the fact that my mother, brother, and sister always wanted to come visit. This made us argue a lot, not to mention Lee wanted to go out all the time like he did in Pittsburgh. All of Lee's focus had been directed toward money, which drove me crazy. Yes, everyone needs money, but this was his obsession, almost like being in love with woman. It made me sick to see Lee act in such a way, not knowing how to handle all my frustrations.

I started drinking beer more and more, at first wanting to express how I felt about him always pleasing himself and not putting effort into the relationship. This made it worse; expressing myself made it seem as if I were a nag. So I then went to drinking beer more than I had before as a way of getting sleep at night after a hard day's work. That is exactly what happened. We both agreed to go to college to have a career instead of just working to get by, thinking that may solve our problems. It worked for a while, but then we went back to the old behaviors.

Lee was going out a lot, enjoying himself but wanting me to stay at home all the time. I really didn't mind staying at home, but the thought of him being out made my skin crawl. Knowing Lee's past was enough to make me feel a certain way about his actions and to trust a man that doesn't trust you made it more upsetting. Lee worked a lot during this time of our relationship, having both a full-time and part-time job, but he stopped working the part-time job to start college. We both graduated after two years of struggling in our relationship while raising Morgan at the same time. It became very difficult for me, though, having to work full time, cook, clean, and do school part time. Oh, I thought about giving up a lot. Lee was always trying to find ways to make me do it all. One thing came after the other until I just got to the point of just going with the flow, not stunting him at all!

In March of 2007, I decided to go and have a breast reduction, thinking this would really help me feel better in a lot of ways. My mother came down to help me, or so I thought. A few days after the surgery, she didn't even want to help me shower. It was a major mind thing, but I was scared to death to even look at my breast. The doctor took six and one half pounds out of me. My recovery didn't go easy at all. One of my breasts took very long to heal. People ask me if I would have it done again, and the answer to that is heck no! No one will ever touch me again unless it is a life-or-death situation due to the complications that were endured.

Lee did take good care of me during my healing process; that is one thing for sure. Needless to say, my mother was still the same when it came to doing anything for me. Suck it up is exactly what I did after going off on her because of her actions. This was one time out of many that she really could have helped me, but two days was enough for her.

After multiple trips back to my surgeon, it was time to go back to work. When I got back, almost everyone just smiled, saying I looked completely different with small breasts. It felt good to wear bras of many colors, and shirts without floral prints, stripes, and odd designs. The job I had at that time was a patient account representative for radiology at the hospital. It was cool for a while, knowing this was not the final place for me. I told Lee that it was time to pursue something more because that school was almost over. This was the perfect time to move around to find a position in my career field that would a descent salary for my bills to be less than what I make instead of my bills being more than what I make.

This didn't sit well for Lee, but it did for me, so I started praying about it. Then I created a fresh resume. I went on Career Builders, the number one job seekers website, and calls started coming in, one after the other. My response to each call was that I only wanted a full-time positions making at least thirty thousand a year or more. It took only a few days to obtain what I desired. This made me know that with prayer and determination you can have what you need in life. Lee became very impressed by my will to strive for the best. After taking the position, I knew it was from the Lord. The position was at a central business office for one of the largest hospitals in Dallas. Everyone on the team I worked with welcomed me and made me feel like family. Of course there are gossipers, haters, and fake people there, but knowing how to play my cards right after all the past positions made this a breeze. I started as a customer service representative for eight months and made my way to a medical biller after graduating during the eight-month period. Life seemed good. My uncle D. moved down here with his wife and stayed with us for a while, but then Lee went off about that. My uncle gave us four hundred dollars a month, so I thought it was all good. This was a major help at the time.

Uncle D. knew Lee was frustrated, so he started looking for an apartment. Then come to find out his wife was just as frustrated too. Uncle D's wife had been a very jealous woman—so jealous that she didn't trust him being my uncle like something else was going on. I told him Lee was crazy, too, so let's just give them what they want: peace in knowing they run the house.

Morgan was thirteen at that time, growing so mature with long legs and arms like her father and a dark complexion with a bright smile. People would say how much she looked like the both of us. This had been true, and what made it worse is that she has both of our attitudes. Boy, our household needed much prayer. Morgan really shocked us because her mouth went along with the attitude. Lee was always upset about it, and all I could do is look back at me. It was a reflection just like looking in the mirror. I got on her about it, but she was stubborn and rebellious to a degree. Life here in Texas has surely been a life full of living for me.

Chapter 13

The Wedding

July 6, 2007 was the day we arrived in Las Vegas. Lee had never been there, so this was a very good trip to take. We planned to get married in Vegas, and that is exactly what we did. A chapel was already reserved for July 7, 2007, with a limo coming to get us from the hotel room that morning. It made us feel like a king and queen. The day we arrived, Lee and I had to stand in a line for three hours just to obtain a marriage license due to all three thousand-plus couples getting married on that day. After waiting so long, we both felt marriage counseling was no longer needed. We both were so excited to go back to the hotel, and I put on some sexy attire for my husband to be. Then we gambled until the club opened up. The club had three floors with different kinds of music, and of course, we went straight to the hip-hop section to get our dance on. After the club, it was time for a couple hours of sleep to prepare for our wedding, and Lee wanted to make love before we were married.

I wasn't with doing that, so I told him, "No, this one night you will wait." Lee never was good with a woman taking control and was upset at first but then realized the next time it would be with his wife. The morning sun crept through our window of the Stratosphere Hotel, so we arose. We felt the sun's glare over our faces to get ready for the special moment. The limo guy called to tell us he would be arriving at 8:15 a.m. Lee and I took our showers, helped each other get dressed, and then went down to the casino floor entrance to await our driver. The ceremony went very fast, but after all I was now Mrs. Lee, looking like the queen of Las Vegas when we got back to the hotel. I kept my dress on and sat at the blackjack table where I won several times. Then we went strolling through Vegas and took a ride in the boat at the Venetian. This was a day to remember for the rest of our lives.

I am his one soulmate, the only one to get into that special place. Boy, does he give up a very good fight! At the end of the day, he is always with me, his wife Mrs. Lee. When we returned, we were greeted by his two daughters along with my niece Nay. They didn't go with us, which turned out to be really a blessing because we had no distractions. I wanted a big wedding, although it couldn't be done due to our families living so far away. Along with expenses for both families, we just wouldn't have been able to afford a big wedding. Neither would they, so Lee and I decided to just go. Now when I look back, there is not one regret with doing it just the two of us. There were no distractions, haters, or nonsupporters around, which made every moment flow the way it was supposed to. I was the bride and my husband the groom, and getting all the attention from one another was a blessing.

This was a relationship neither one of us thought would ever be again, so take a look at us now! Life seemed to be so wonderful as a new wife to my child's father, only to realize this was just the beginning of a whole new hand of cards that was being dealt. The first year of marriage was amazing, but then all the expectations started to arise from the both of us. Marriage is more than just saying I do. The next chapter of my life has a whole new stack of cards that will be shared through Part 2 of Playing the Hand I was Dealt.

9 781498 493093